Reprint Publishing

FOR PEOPLE WHO GO FOR ORIGINALS.

www.reprintpublishing.com

[See p. 73

"I HEARD YOU LUL-LOVED DUD-DANCING,
PRUDENCE, DEAR"

The Worsted Man

A Musical Play for Amateurs

By

John Kendrick Bangs

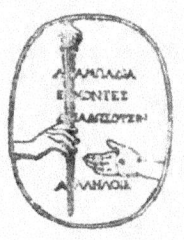

Harper & Brothers Publishers
New York and London
1905

NOTE

The Worsted Man is easily constructed of meagre materials, such as Afghans, sweaters, golf-vests, tam-o'-shanters, worsted mittens, and other simple paraphernalia usually obtainable at any so-called New York store within driving distance of most summer hotels. The hearts may be made of red flannel, maroon velvet, or plain calico, as easily as bean-bags. They should be stuffed with corn-meal, absorbent cotton, or some equally impressionable material, in order to give them a suitable masculine flexibility. The music throughout is from the best-known comic operas of Messrs. Gilbert and Sullivan, the scores of which are

iii

Note

to be had of most live music dealers and of some dead ones. An effort has been made to choose the simplest numbers, so that the musical requirements of the operetta shall present no serious obstacle in the way of the amateur singer or accompanist. In the Incantation Scene the action calls for thunder, but this is not essential to the plot, and may be omitted in case there are no small boys around to raise it.

J. K. B.

ILLUSTRATIONS

THE CAST

MR. WOOLLEY, *The Worsted Man, A Doll, An Expedient, and A Flirt.*

MISS PATIENCE WILLOUGHBY, *An Ingenious Young Woman, known as Impatience for an obvious reason.*

MISS MARIANNA JONES, *A Summer Girl, willing to be wooed.*

MISS BABETTE HAWKINS, *Another, anxious to be courted.*

MISS JANETTE BARRINGTON, *A third, desirous of being won.*

MISS SUSANNA DARROW, *A fourth, not averse to gallantry.*

MISS PRISCILLA MIDDLETON, *A fifth, looking for a cavalier.*

MISS PRUDENCE ANDREWS, *A sixth, with her cap set.*

The Cast

Miss Ethelinda De Witt, *A seventh,
except in years, where she is easily first,
being quite thirty-seven; ready for
anything.*
Sambo Front, Esq., *A Bell-Boy of ebon hue.
Clerks, Waitresses, Porters, One Invalid, and other Characters who may
be introduced at random as long
as they do not speak.
Also one competent pianist to serve in place of
an orchestra.*

vii

THE WORSTED MAN

SCENE I.—*The Office of a Summer Hotel at Highland Hills, New Hampshire.*

It is one of those comfortably arranged offices that does duty at the height of the season as a gathering-place for guests after breakfast and dinner, where men may smoke if there are any to smoke and they wish to do so, and the women assemble to put sofa-cushions, embroidered centre-pieces, knitted golf-vests, and other things together while pulling reputations apart. The walls are decorated with lithographed ideals of other summer hotels in distant parts of the country, advertisements of railways, time-tables, and portraits of imaginary trout that were not caught in the adjacent streams. At right is elevator. At left is huge, open fireplace. At rear

3

The Worsted Man

is desk for cashier, registry, etc. All the clerks are women. There is one colored bell-boy, who also runs the elevator. Above the mantel-piece the head of a moose shot eight hundred miles from the hotel is affixed to the chimney-breast and gazes placidly through its glass eyes upon all that goes on within range of their sockets. The action of non-speaking characters in the play is continuous—porters carrying in trunks, the elevator incessantly running, the cashier footing-up columns of figures and chewing upon the end of her penholder; an occasional waitress passes through, carrying a large tray holding teacups, teapots, dishes of milk-toast, etc. The only masculine life in sight consists of the colored bell-boy and an octogenarian invalid who for the sake of verisimilitude in the play is frequently rolled across the rear of the stage in a wicker wheel-chair.

4

The Worsted Man

Curtain rising discloses seven Summer Girls sitting in a group, sewing, knitting, and embroidering.

Time—A brilliant morning in mid-August.

Opening Chorus

(Music: That of Opening Chorus of "Patience.")

Seven lone lorn maidens we,
    Not a man to ease our woe.
All the season we shall be
    Seven lone lorn maidens—oh!

Solo: Marianna

Love feeds on hope, they say, or love
    will die,

All

Ah, miserie!

Yet on the bill of fare no hope we spy.

All

Ah, miserie!

5

The Worsted Man

Alas for us, we sit and sadly plan

ALL
Ah, miserie!

A summer in an Eden without man.

ALL
Ah, miserie!

CHORUS
All our love is wasted quite,
    All our yearnings go for naught,
Not a single youth in sight,
    By our glances to be caught!

ALL
Ah, miserie!

SOLO: SUSANNA
Oh, glancing eyes,
    Thy glancing all is wasted!
Oh, starving heart,
    The sweets of love untasted.

"SEVEN LONE LORN MAIDENS WE"

The Worsted Man

Oh, fancy free,
　What boots a fancy flitting
When all thy dreams
　Awake to empty knitting?

ALL

Ah, miserie!

Marianna. Heigho! What a cruel
fate indeed is ours! Wealth, beauty,
talent—everything to make us attractive, and immured here in this nunnery
of the hills! Our watchword, "Nit,"
with or without the K.

Babette. As if we had committed
some awful crime that shuts us out of
men's society forever!

Susanna. If we only had one man, it
would be something.

Marianna. We could have him one
day a week apiece, at least.

Priscilla. Isn't it surprising that our
philanthropic millionaires do not take

up this awful summer - hotel situation instead of endowing libraries and chairs in embroidery at colleges. How much better would seven young men be for us than all the libraries in the world!

Babette. And it wouldn't cost so very much either. Men are so cheap in town.

Janette. That's very true — but a better plan would be for the department stores to take it up. Certainly, if they are to deal in monkeys and parrots, and butter and eggs, there's no reason why they shouldn't have a line of beaux. Then we could telegraph to town and secure a few—on approval, of course.

Prudence. I'd subscribe for a regular weekly service.

Ethelinda. And I, too—a new young man served every Monday, just as they send you books from the Book Fancier's Library.

Janette. I wonder what would happen

if we did wire Dugan & Bunkum for seven young men by return mail.

Prudence. They have better - looking ones at Harris & Peters.

Priscilla. Oh no, Prudence. The Harris & Peters men are so sort of common, don't you think? For perfect gentlemen Wilkins & Jones are—

Susanna. Haven't any of you any brothers we can send for?

Janette. I have one, but he is only seven, and an *enfant terrible* at that. But where is Impatience this morning? She hasn't joined us for three or four days past. What do you suppose she is up to?

Marianna. I haven't an idea—she's so mysterious about her plans. I—

[*The elevator door opens.* IMPA-
TIENCE *emerges.*

Impatience. Good - morning, every - body. Anybody lend me a *fiancé* this morning? It's a glorious day for a walk.

The Worsted Man

Babette. It ill becomes you, Impatience, just because you have no particular liking for men to twit us—

Impatience. Twit you, Babette? Never. I sympathize with you all, but moping will not help. Action—action, that is what the emergency demands. (*Mysteriously*). Sh! Girls—come here —come close. I've a plan!

[*All rise and group themselves about* Impatience.

SOLO: IMPATIENCE

(*Music: "The Policemen's Chorus," from "Pirates of Penzance."*)

When there's something that you lack,
      Tarantara, Tarantara!
And your heart has gone to wrack,
      Tarantara!
Don't sit down and merely mope,
      Tarantara, Tarantara!
And give up all earthly hope—

The Worsted Man

ALL
(*Visibly brightening.*)

Tarantara!

IMPATIENCE

When you cannot find the thing
      Tarantara, tarantara!
That will surest surcease bring—

ALL

(*Softly smiling.*)

Tarantara!

IMPATIENCE

Why go in and promptly act,
      Tarantara, tarantara!
Till the thing you seek's a fact!
      Tarantara!

OMNES

Tarantara-ra-ra-ra-ra!
Tarantara-ra-ra-ra-ra!

The Worsted Man

ALL

We'll go in and promptly act,
Till the thing we seek's a fact—
   Tarantara, tarantara-ra-ra-ra-ra!

IMPATIENCE

Now that's what I have done,
     Tarantara, tarantara!
And there's going to be some fun,
     Tarantara!
I have settled on a plan—

ALL

(Eagerly.)
Tarantara, tarantara?

IMPATIENCE

That will give us all a *man*—

ALL

(Enthusiastically.)
Tarantara!

12

The Worsted Man

IMPATIENCE

I've devised a little scheme—

ALL

(*Inquiringly.*)

Tarantara, tarantara?

IMPATIENCE

That will prove a perfect dream—

ALL

(*Hopefully.*)

Tarantara!

IMPATIENCE

If it works out as it should—

ALL

(*Expectant.*)

Tarantara, tarantara!

IMPATIENCE

It should be—(*hesitates*)—well, pretty
    good—

Tarantara—

The Worsted Man

ALL

(*Hurriedly.*)
Tarantara-ra-ra-ra-ra!
Tarantara-ra-ra-ra-ra!

OMNES

We'll accept it as we should,
If it turns out pretty good—
Tarantara, tarantara-ra-ra-ra-ra!

Priscilla. But what *is* your scheme,
Impatience? You cannot charm us
with a song, you know, even if we have
joined in the chorus. We have music
a-plenty, but of schemes—

Impatience. It is simple enough.
Have you read the prospectus of this
hotel?

All. Yes.

Priscilla. But it says nothing about
men. Excellent cuisine, golf-links,
music, and beautiful drives in the neigh-

borhood, but, alas! no promise of male society.

Marianna. In fact, everything but the thing we most desire. Who cares for nineteen different kinds of hot bread for breakfast, with no beaux at the hops?

Janette. Or for magnificent views from the surrounding hills without a pair of man's eyes to share them?

Babette. Or long sylvan walks—alone! With nothing to talk to but the chipmunks and the birds—

Impatience. (*Laughing.*) How sad, indeed, your unhappy fate—so sad that you have overlooked the great promise of the waters.

All. The waters?

Babette. You speak in riddles, Impatience.

Impatience. You are so blinded by your woes you will not see. But listen. (*Takes circular from her pocket and reads.*)

15

"But it is of the waters of the Highland Hills we would chiefly speak. Who that has tasted them but becomes ever after their stanchest champion? Healthful, invigorating, life-giving. Read some of the testimonials."

Babette. Oh, dear — what waste of time, Impatience!

Impatience. (*Reading.*) "The Rectory, Pikefarm Corners, N. J., August 30, 1904. Gentlemen:—Permit me to thank you for the case of Highland Hill water received last week. It is all that you claim for it. I was prostrated, nerveless, unable to move, to think, to speak, or to act. One quart of your wonderful water has put me on my feet again. In fact, it has brought me to life. Send two more cases at once, C. O. D. Yours, always faithfully, Rev. Wilberforce Hicks-Wiggs."

Janette. Well—what of it?

Impatience. Oh, how dull! The man's

a minister. He wouldn't try to deceive anybody, would he?

All. No.

Impatience. Well — if the water brought him to life, why wouldn't it bring—another man to life? Indeed, this circular is full of similar letters. Highland Hill water gives life to all.

Babette. But what man? You've got to have some raw material to work on, Impatience. There isn't even a dead one in this neighborhood.

Impatience. (*Running to rear and securing a huge bundle, which she brings back to front.*) I have been busy for four days, Babette—doing—what do you suppose, Marianna?

　　[*Cuts string and begins to tear wrapper away.*

All. (*Eagerly.*) What is it?

Impatience. This!

　　[*Jerks huge worsted doll from parcel,*

17

and dangles it by the neck before them.

All. A worsted man?

Impatience. The very same. Let me introduce him. Ladies, may I present Mr.—er—ah—Mr. Woolley, of—er—Afghanistan. Mr. Woolley, my friends—Miss Marianna Jones, Miss Babette Hawkins, Miss Janette Barrington, Miss Susanna Darrow, Miss Priscilla Middleton, Miss Prudence Andrews, and Miss Ethelinda De Witt — likewise, your most humble servant, Patience Willoughby, generally known as Impatience.

[*All courtesy.* IMPATIENCE *bobs doll at each.*

Ethelinda. What lovely eyes! They have all the sparkling vivacity of a pair of shoe-buttons.

Babette. He hasn't much conversation, has he?

Susanna. (*Squeezing doll's arm.*) He's a dream of beauty—but a trifle soft for me.

The Worsted Man

Marianna. Where *did* you get this fascinating cavalier, Impatience?

Impatience. Made him — knitted him myself, while you girls were moping.

Priscilla. And why? I, for one, do not care for dolls.

Impatience. Wait until we have cast a spell upon him. (*Draws up an arm-chair to centre of stage.*) Will your majesty please be seated? (*Places doll in arm-chair, face to audience, hands out-stretched on arm of chair.*) Now, Mr. Front, a glass of fresh spring-water, please.

Bell-Boy. Yassum. Hot or cold? Wet or dry? With or without?

Impatience. Without — delay, Mr. Front—fresh from the spring—therefore cold—in fact, the kind that gives life.

Bell-Boy. Yassum. (*Aside.*) It's rotten water. When I drink it, it makes me want to woyk. (*Exit. Music of*

The Worsted Man

incantation, pianissimo, until boy re-
turns with glass of water, which he hands
to Impatience.) Dere's enough water in
dat glass to raise all Egyp'!

IMPATIENCE

(Improvised recitative, tragically.)
Let every maid
Who feels afraid—
At heart—

Let every one
Who'd like to run,
Depart.

The things we'll see
May horrid be,
I tell you at the start.

[*Lights grow dim.* IMPATIENCE *ad-*
vances to worsted doll and places
glass at its lips.

"'DERE'S ENOUGH WATER IN DAT GLASS TO RAISE ALL EGYP'!"

The Worsted Man

SONG: IMPATIENCE

*(Music: " Incantation," etc., from " The
Sorcerer.")*

Spirits of the hills,
Fiends of mountain-tops,
All ye snakes
And other fakes,
And all ye rural fops—
Come down, come down, come down!

VOICES

(From without.)
We've just arrived from town!

IMPATIENCE

All ye loathsome things—
Spiders, pugs, and hags,
Hill-top churls
With yellow curls,
Rigged out in gladdest rags—
Come down, come down, come down!

The Worsted Man

Voices

(From without.)
We're here to do it brown.

Marianna

(Fearsomely.)
Hist! They are coming!—
Those fiends of the hills.

Babette

(Comfortingly.)
'Tis only the humming
Of unpaid bills!

Aria: Impatience

Let us ask of the kindly fates,
　Who guard us with friendly eye,
That on what the prospectus states
　We may surely all rely:
That a glass of this water cold,
　On this plainly printed plan,
Will transform this worsted mould
　To a palpitating man.

22

The Worsted Man

CHORUS OF SPIRITS

'Tis done, 'tis done—
　　You have your way.
Now for the fun
　　And light of day.

IMPATIENCE, MARIANNA, AND BABETTE

'Tis done, 'tis done,
　　We have our way!
May it be fun
　　And not dismay!

IMPATIENCE

Ye mountain heights and piney flights,
　　Ye pollywogs and bears,
Ye unpaid bills and towering hills,
　　Ye lame piazza chairs,
Ye powdered mas and henpecked pas,
　　And other parlor tricks,
Smile on our plan to make this man,
　　And ease our summer fix.

23

The Worsted Man

[*Pouring water into mouth of Worsted Man.*
Drink the first!

ALL
'Tis the worst!

IMPATIENCE
(*Repeating operation.*)
Drink the tooth!

ALL
Sorry youth!

IMPATIENCE
(*Ditto.*)
Drink the third!

ALL
Hath occurred.

VOICES
(*From without.*)
Hath occurred, now let us see,
Ha-ha-ha!
What comes out of number three,
Ha-ha-ha!

24

The Worsted Man

BABETTE AND MARIANNA
(*Aside.*)
We have prayed to the kindly fates,
Who guard us with kindly eye,
And on what the prospectus states,
We fear we must now rely.
                    [*Stage goes wholly dark.*

VOICES

(*From all points of the compass.*)
Ha! ha! ha! ha! ha! ha! ha! ha! ha! ha!
*There is a roll of thunder, a flash
of lightning, and stage becomes
brilliant again. The young ladies
stand back somewhat awed,* IM-
PATIENCE *slightly to the fore, gazing
in rapt astonishment at the worsted
doll, which, sitting in the chair,
has suddenly come to life.*

THE DOLL
(*Blinking his eyes and gazing about him
in amazement.*)

3   25

The Worsted Man

Where am I at, and what's my name?
Is this all real or just a game?

IMPATIENCE

You are a man, a worsted man,
Constructed from an old Afghan,
And stuffed with cotton, rags, and bran.

THE DOLL

(*With a grin.*)
And you—
Art worsted too?
[*Springs forward to seize her.* IM-
PATIENCE *eludes him, and he
begins a shuffling dance, and
song.*

SONG: THE WORSTED MAN

(*Music: "I'm a Most Intense Young
Man," from "Patience."*)
Oh I am a worsted man,
I'm made of an old Afghan,

26

The Worsted Man

Embroidered with botany,
Stuffed with a cottony
Mixture of rags and bran.

Chorus

Oh, the worsted worsted man,
A most original man,
Embroidered with botany,
Brains—he's not got any,
Rotteny, cottony man.

The Doll

I'm a limply limber man,
A toes-made-of-timber man,
And though made of zephyr, I
Dance like a heifer—I
Only just now began.

Chorus

Oh the timber-toed young man,
Oh the gawky-walky man,

The Worsted Man

A flippity-floppity
Hippity-hoppity
Double loose-jointed man.

Doll. Well, ladies, this is an unexpected pleasure. I had no idea last evening, when my fair friend Miss Impatience here was sewing my eyes in and putting the finishing touches to my ears, and manicuring my mittens, that to-day would find me a living creature like the rest of you, instead of that genial but unintelligent bit of creation known to history as an Afghan.

Priscilla. Are your eyes really sewed in?

Doll. Yes, Miss Priscilla, with cotton thread.

Marianna. And can you see through them?

Doll. No, ma'am. They are made of shoe-buttons, which are not transparent. But I can see through the

28

little button-holes by which they are
surrounded.

Babette. And — Mr. Woolley — have
you—have you a—heart?

Doll. A which?

Janette. A heart—

Doll. Never heard of such a thing.
What's it like—an automobile?

Impatience. Something.   It goes of its
own power, at least.

Doll. And is all the time blowing up,
and running off at a tangent, and
bumping into something and raising hob
generally?

Marianna. A perfect description of a
heart, Mr. Woolley.

Doll. Really?   Well — no, I haven't
one, but I'd like a few.   If you'll kindly
direct me to the heart shop, and—er—
lend me a dollar, I'll get one for myself,
and maybe buy some for each of you.

Impatience. Hearts are not bought—
they are won.

Doll. Then I will play the game to win one. What is it?

Impatience. (*Demurely.*) The game of love.

Doll. Love?

Impatience. Love.

Doll. My! What a lot of nice new things I am finding to-day. This world seems a pretty good sort of place. Do you know, I like that word love — it conveys an idea to my absorbent-cotton brains; it gives a strange thrill to the bright particular wad of rags with which my left side is stuffed; it brings to these shoe-buttons of mine—

All. These what?

Doll. These shoe-buttons—oh, I forgot. I should have said these eyes of mine. It brings to these eyes of mine a soft and sheepish feeling which un-decides me as to whether I should crack my calico lips by smiling till I break the thread that binds my ears to my pillowy head or fray my button-hole coign of vision by the shedding of an excelsior tear.

Babette. (*Aside.*) He is simply fascinating.

Marianna. Shakespeare could be no worse.

Janette. If his brains are cotton, send me a man with a bale.

Ethelinda. Ain't he grand!

Doll. Have any of you ladies got hearts?

Impatience. All of us have them.

Doll. Lend me a few — just to play with, won't you? You certainly don't all need them this morning, do you?

Marianna. Hearts are not to be played with, Mr. Woolley. But tell us —what is your notion of love?

Doll. Love? Well, let me see— (*reflecting*)—love is a mystery, eh? It is to me, anyhow. But as I think about it, it's like this:

31

The Worsted Man

SONG: THE DOLL

*(Music: "If You Want a Receipt," from
"Patience.")*

If you want a receipt for that popular
    mystery,
  Known to the world as the "Passion
    of Love,"
Take all the romances in newspaper
    history,
  Whether they come from below or
    above,
The dash of a writer enamoured of
    "royalty,"
  Genius of bosses devising a "coup,"
The notions of Arnold, when speaking
    of "loyalty,"
  This for the lover who isn't quite
    true!—
The science of Darwin, the eminent
    monkeyite—
  Wit that's spontaneous, fresh from
    the zoo—

32

The Worsted Man

Plus the devotion of Jeems—such a
    flunkyite
    Maid with a sentiment "wholly for
      you,"
Feeling of Carvel for Mister George
    Washington,
Matinée idols in rôle of Lord Sloshington,
Love of the Kaiser for statecraft delec-
    table,
Passion of Edward for life that's re-
    spectable,
    Magazine poetry, moves for reform,
    Any old thing that is easy and warm,
Take of these elements very confusible,
Melt 'em all up in a thing indeducible,
Let 'em boil down, and then skim from
    above,
And the prize of the effort is love, love,
    love.

CHORUS

Yes, yes, yes, yes,
The prize of the effort is love, love, love.

33

The Worsted Man

Babette. You are a pessimist, Mr. Woolley.

Doll. Not I. Listen. (*Sings.*)

If you're seeking another receipt for this
    sentiment,
  Cherished by all men, from Adam to
    Bill—
The Kaiser of Germany, he is the gent I
    meant—
  Men of the tropics or arctical chill;
Take all the affections, the brother
    and sistery;
  Feeling of Jacky for dear little Jill;
Caress of a plaster that's luridly blistery;
  Joy of a nightingale trilling her trill;
The pride of a mother when bright little
    brotherkin
Plays a rich joke on his uncle or other
    kin;
Smile of a father, a trifle hysterical,
Watching his hopeful when kicking the
    spherical

The Worsted Man

Strenuous pigskin direct for the goal;
Bliss of a beggar when munching a
    roll;
Take of these elements highly delec-
    table,
Leave out whatever is not quite re-
    spectable,
Let 'em boil down, and then skim from
    above,
And the prize of the effort is love, love,
    love.

CHORUS

Yes, yes, yes, yes,
The prize of the effort is love, love, love.

Impatience. That is far better, Mr.
Woolley. Your intuitions as to love
are pretty reliable, but you cannot avail
yourself of them unless you have a
heart. I cannot give you mine—no,
nor even lend it to you, for it is far away.
In fact, it has already been played for
and won. But these other maidens,

35

they all have them — large, beautiful, roomy hearts, which may be won if you only play according to the rules.

Doll. According to the rules, eh?
Impatience. Yes — let me tell you what is my idea of love, and then — then you will better understand. (*Sings.*)

SONG: IMPATIENCE

(*Music: "I Cannot Tell What This Love May Be," from "Patience."*)
I'll tell you about this sentiment
That moveth the world to some extent:
It cometh to all in some queer form;
Sometimes it is cold, sometimes it's warm.
It bringeth to one but deep regret,
It filleth with bliss another yet;
To some it is pain, to others joy,
To some it is gold, to some alloy.
    But everywhere true love you'll see,
    It cometh to you, it comes to me,
    No matter at all where we may be—

The Worsted Man

And that is why we gayly smile:
True love is with us all the while.
Love is the watchword, land or sea—
Fal-la-la-la, fal-la-la-lee!

CHORUS

Yes, that is why we gayly smile:
True love is with us all the while.
Love is the watchword, land or sea—
Fal-la-la-la, fal-la-la-lee!

IMPATIENCE

Some call it a thorn, but they don't
    know;
Some think it as icy as the snow;
Some scamper away when love appears;
Some greet him with smiles and some
    with tears.
But love is a painter, soft of mien,
Who painteth the sere and yellow green;
It dwelleth deep in the maiden's heart,
And springeth to life from Cupid's dart.

37

The Worsted Man

And everywhere true love you'll see:
It cometh to birdlings in the tree,
To beasts of the field and forest free;
  And that is why the glad world
    smiles,
    For love is with it every whiles.
    Love is a watchword, land or sea—
    Fal-la-la-la, fal-la-la-lee!

Chorus

Yes, that is why the glad world smiles,
For love is with it every whiles.
Love is a watchword, land or sea—
Fal-la-la-la, fal-la-la-lee!

Doll. Well, I suppose I ought to understand. And I think I would if you hadn't stuffed my head full of excelsior instead of brains. But it doesn't make any difference whether I understand love or not—what is clear is that I must have a heart to keep it in.

Impatience. That's it.

The Worsted Man

Doll. Just as an automobile has to have a tank to keep the gasoline in.

Babette. You've got it.

Doll. Or a billionaire has to have a check-book to keep his money in.

Marianna You think remarkably well with that excelsior gray matter of yours, Mr. Woolley.

Ethelinda. Ain't he grand!

Doll. And then there are rules for this game of love.

Babette. Unless you are a flirt, Mr. Woolley.

Doll. A flirt? What is a flirt? It sounds rather attractive.

Impatience. (*Aside.*) How imprudent of you, Babette, to mention such a thing in the presence of this child of zephyr! (*Severely, to the Doll.*) A flirt is a robber—a bandit—a burglar who breaks into the bank of love and steals away its treasures that he may squander them. A flirt is a bankrupt in con-

science who issues notes of affection at
ninety days, discounts them, and fails
to pay at maturity. A flirt is a pro-
moter who incorporates the heart into
a stock company and issues shares to
the amount of a hundred times its
value and unloads upon the confiding
public at par, defaults on his interest,
and when the stock falls to eleven and
an eighth condones his offence by
making large gifts of philanthropy to
the community—

Doll. My! but that sounds nice.

Janette. Nice? Nice? Really, Impatience, I fear you've put a lump of
shoddy in where Mr. Woolley's con-
science should have been.

Doll. But aren't flirts nice? Don't
people trust them? It must be nice to
be trusted.

Impatience. Oh, dear, but this is a
hard case. That's just the trouble, Mr.
Woolley—people do trust them—

Babette. But they don't play according to the rules.

Doll. Ah, I see. And not to play according to the rules—that is wrong?

Impatience. Very—and those who don't are punished severely. IF WE FIND YOU FLIRTING, MR. WOOLLEY, WE'LL — WE'LL — WELL, WE'LL (DESPERATELY) UNRAVEL YOU!

> [WOOLLEY *shrinks back in dismay.*

Doll. (*Hoarsely.*) The rules — the rules. Such an awful fate! Oh, the rules, Impatience, the rules.

(*Improvised recitative.*)

Oh prithee, ma'am, give me the rules
That must prevail in Cupid's schools,
And I'll obey, I promise thee,
Lest I should bear the penalty,
And, horror! should unravelled be.

4

The Worsted Man

IMPATIENCE

Now listen ye,
We'll tell it thee,
The single rule
Of Cupid's school.
Alas! Alack! Ah, well-a-day
For you if this you disobey.

IMPATIENCE, DOLL, AND CHORUS
(*Music: "True Love Must Single-Hearted Be," from "Patience."*)

IMPATIENCE

True love must single-hearted be.

CHORUS

Exactly so.

IMPATIENCE

Free from all vile duplicity.

DOLL

Exactly so.

42

The Worsted Man

IMPATIENCE

No empty sighs to mystify;
No promises framed but to die.
True love, indeed, will never die.

ALL

Exactly so.

IMPATIENCE

One maid alone for every heart.

CHORUS

Exactly so.

IMPATIENCE

One maid alone for Cupid's dart.

DOLL

Exactly so.

IMPATIENCE

No heart for two, or three, or four.
No heart with first and second floor
No heart divided 'mong a score.

The Worsted Man

ALL

Exactly so.

[*Girls form ring around* DOLL *and
commence dancing and singing.*

True love must single-hearted be.

Exactly so.

Free from all vain frivolity.

Exactly so.

One heart for one, one for each heart,

That is the true true-lover's part

When in Dan Cupid's busy mart.

Exactly so.

CURTAIN.

SCENE II.—*The same. Worsted Man on alone, save for the clerks, hall-boy, etc.*

SONG: THE DOLL

SORRY HIS LOT THAT LOVES BUT ONE

(*Music: "Sorry Her Lot Who Loves Too Well," from "Pinafore."*)

Sorry his lot that loves but one.
  Heavy the soul that hopes but singly.
Black are the heavens, and dark the sun,
    Dashed from his throne is Cupid
      kingly.
      Deep is the heartache that racks
      the breast,
      Fired for one and chilled for the
      rest.
Drear is the hour, and gray the day,
  Arid and waste as vast Sahara,

45

The Worsted Man

When one turns back from Jane and
    May
  And Sue and Prue and Kate for
    Sarah!
    Deep is the heartache that racks
    the breast,
    Fired for one and chilled for the rest.

(*Sighs.*) Heigho! I know not what I
shall do. As yet I have no heart, and
as for my excelsior mind, it is racked
with doubt. The law says flirt not on
pain of unravelment, and yet how can I
deny my smiles to Marianna while
beaming pleasantly on Babette? Why
should I call Marianna sweetheart while
casting an icy shoe-button—I, ah, should
say eye—on fair Priscilla? Why should
the cotton pulse beneath my zephyr
wristlets beat madly for Priscilla and
remain unmoved when I feel the soft
pressure of Janette's hand upon my
mitts? Alas, I know not what to do!

46

The Worsted Man

[*Buries face in his hands—bell rings in office.*

Bell-Boy. (*To front.*) D'joo ring, suh.

Doll. Ring? Me? No. What do you mean? What would I ring for?

Bell-Boy. (*Grinning.*) One o' de customs ob de country, suh. Folks most generally rings de bell, suh, when dey wants somepin.

Doll. Ah — I see. Well, my boy, I do want something. I want to find a way out of this predicament I am in.

Bell-Boy. Dis ain't no prediggament, suh. Dis am a hotel.

Doll. Suppose, my lad, that I should find myself wanting something, and I rang that bell to which you refer, would I be likely to get it?

Bell-Boy. In co'se you would, suh. Das what I'm hyar foh.

Doll. Even if it were a—a—a heart?

Bell-Boy. (*Laughing outright.*) Lord bres yo, suh. Hearts is de easiest

47

thing in de woyld to get in a place like dis in de summah - time. I got a box full ob 'em up-stairs in my room, suh, left over from last summah.

Doll. Left over from last summer?

Bell-Boy. Yassir. You see, suh, folks is mighty careless ob deir hearts in de summah-time. Dey cyarries 'em around on deir sleeves an' dey leaves 'em about kind o' permiskious like. Dere's no end ob 'em gits lost, an' de queer part ob it is dat de folks what loses 'em ain't willin' to let on dey's done lost 'em. Las' year, when de hotel shet up foh de season, I foun' ten ob 'em lyin' roun' dis hyar place. One out in de woods; one ob 'em up on de mountain-side; two ob 'em floatin' roun' on de soyface ob de lake, three ob 'em in de summah-house down by de spring; two ob 'em in de dinin'-room, an' one corkin' big feller lyin' 'longside de seventh hole on de golf-links.

The Worsted Man

Doll. (*Amazed.*)   And their owners?

Bell-Boy. Oh, we nebber could tell who dey belonged to.   Wouldn't even pay foh to advertise 'em, suh.   Owners wouldn't have de noyve to come an' ast for 'em, suh.   So I jes' put 'em away in a big pasteboard box wid a han'ful o' camphor-balls to keep de moths out, an' lef' 'em in my quarters all winter long.   Like to buy one, suh?   I'll let 'em go cheap—dollah apiece, suh.

Doll. (*Dancing with joy.*)   Ten of them did you say, boy?

Bell-Boy. Yassir—one ob 'em's a little frayed roun' de edges, an' two ob 'em's a bit cracked, suh, but in general dey's a pretty fair lot o' hearts, suh.

Doll. Bring them here.

Bell-Boy. Very good, suh.   [*Exit.*

Doll. Ten hearts!   Ten hearts!   I seem to have struck a heart-mine in that chocolate - faced menial.   Let me see, that will be one for each—Babette,

Marianna, Impatience, Janette, Ethelinda, Susanna, Prudence, and Priscilla (*counting on his fingers*), and two left over for an emergency. Good! It's always well to have something in reserve. And, best of all, I shall not be accused of flirting! (*Sings.*)

True love must single-hearted be—
      Exactly so.
Free from all vain frivolity—
      Exactly so.
One heart for one, one for each heart—
That is the true true-lover's part
When in Dan Cupid's busy mart.
      Ahem! Just so.
        [*Enter* BELL-BOY *with box.*

Doll. Hail, my chestnut Cupid! Hast brought the goods?

Bell-Boy. Dat I hast, suh.

Doll. Then haste thee, Dan, and let me see them.

      [BELL-BOY *removes cover from box*

and takes out several heart-shaped objects, which he hands to WOOLLEY.

Bell-Boy. Dey's de straight articles, suh. All sizes, an' warranted not to crock or fade.

[WOOLLEY *looks them carefully over, and places each in a different pocket as he completes his inspection. During action the following dialogue.*

Doll. This one appears to be cracked.

Bell-Boy. Yassir, but dat doan' make no difference. Dere's not many hearts dese days dat hav'n't had some kind ob a knock, an' some ob 'em's mighty brittle. (*Handling one of them in gingerly fashion.*) Look out foh dat one, Mistuh Woolley. Yo' may boyn yo' fingahs.

Doll. (*Taking it from bell - boy.*) Jerusalem! (*Nearly drops it.*) It is pretty warm, isn't it?

Bell-Boy. (*Handing him another.*) Dis

yere one's done been scorched a bit, but it woyks all right.

Doll. It's pretty cold though, now.

Bell-Boy. Yassir. Das de trouble wid dese scorched ones—dey cools off arter a while—das what dey calls de marble heart, suh. Look at dis yere, Mistuh Woolley. (*Holds up a heart about three times as large as the rest.*) Ain't dat a winner? It's one o' dem hotel hearts.

Doll. Hotel hearts, boy?

Bell-Boy. Yassir, big enough to hold an excoysion party.

Doll. It's a beauty. (*Holding it up admiringly.*) I should have thought its owner would have reclaimed it, it's so exceptionally large and roomy.

Bell-Boy. I guess he must o' been a Mormon and didn't want to let on. (*Pauses.*) Well, dar dey is. Yo' can take your pick foh a dollar, suh.

Doll. How much for the lot?

"AIN'T DAT A WINNER? IT'S ONE O' DEM
HOTEL HEARTS"

Bell - Boy. (*Aghast.*) What — all ob 'em, Mistuh Woolley? What yo' gwine do wid ten hearts?

Doll. Oh—I may have need for them. I'll give you seven fifty for the lot.

Bell-Boy. Say eight and dey's yours.

Doll. Done! Have them put on my bill, and, mind you, not a word to anybody.

> [*Enter* IMPATIENCE. WOOLLEY *hastily hides last heart inside his waistcoat.*

Bell-Boy. All right, Mistuh Woolley. I'll hab de ice-water up right away, suh. [*Exit.*

Impatience. Let me warn you, Mr. Woolley, not to drink too much of these waters. They are very powerful and they *may* make you—flirt. I have already told you (*severely*) what will happen if you—flirt.

Doll. I know the rule, Miss. One heart —one love. Is that it?

53

The Worsted Man

Impatience. You have learned the lesson well. That's exactly it. And if you have—no heart—no love.

Doll. And how about ten hearts? Ten loves?

Impatience. Don't be absurd, Mr. Woolley. We sometimes find four-handed men and six-legged calves among the freaks of the circus, but as yet a ten-hearted man—oh, well, its nonsense. It's getting so these days that it is not easy to find a man with one heart, much less ten. The sex seems to be all taken up with automobiles, golf-clubs, rackets, clubs, and sometimes business. Phyllis mourns her Strephon, whose days are spent on the links. Beatrice sits at home—an automobile widow. Penelope enjoyed the society of Ulysses as much as nowadays we women enjoy that of our husbands, brothers, *fiancés*, and friends. It is preposterous. (*Sings.*)

The Worsted Man

MEN AND HEARTS. BALLAD

(*Music: "Time Was When Love and I Were Well Acquainted," from "The Sorcerer."*)

Time was when men and hearts were
    found together;
  Time was when dainty Cupid found a
    nest,
To shelter him from storm and wintry
    weather,
  Within the stronghold of some manly
    breast.
But now, alas! poor Dan—sad little
    laddy—
  Finds, 'stead of hearts to shelter him
    galore,
A golf club where he has to act as caddy,
  And pace the wind-swept golf-links
    keeping score!

No longer do the lads pursue the lasses,
  But chase by night and day some
    pewter mug.

The Worsted Man

The motor-car, perfumed with noxious
    gases.
    Alone doth set their heart-strings all
      a-chug.
And now, alas! poor Dan—sad little
    duffer—
    Finds, 'stead of hearts to shelter him
      from pain,
That he must act as some cold master's
    "chuffer,"
    And guide his motor-car through sun
      and rain.

Ah, Strephon! What a change has come
    upon you
    That you should leave man's best gift
      in the lurch!
Pray, whither have your ancient man-
    ners gone—you
    No more escort your heart's desire to
      church?
Oh, what, alas! has Dan—poor little
    Cupid—

What has he done that you should
    treat him thus?
The fashion seems to me so very stupid,
    And from some points of view pre-
    posterous.

Doll. And is that why, when you constructed me, you left out my heart?
(*Reproachfully.*) Did you wish me to
be as preposterous as all the rest?
Impatience. I intended to give you
one later, as soon as I was convinced
that you were capable of using it properly. We do not permit children to
play with fire-arms until they have been
taught to handle them. When you
have shown your fitness to possess a
heart, Mr. Woolley, you shall have
one.
Doll. (*Gleefully.*) But I have, I
have, I have. I already have one.
    [*Dances joyously about the stage,
        holding the large heart high in*

The Worsted Man

the air. IMPATIENCE *starts back in amazed dismay.*

Impatience. Where — where did you get it? Come—tell me.

Doll. (*In sing-song voice.*) The fairies, the fairies brought it to me. (*Points it at her.*) Isn't it a beauty?

Impatience. (*Holding up her hands in horror.*) Look out—hearts are dangerous. It may go off at any minute—

Doll. This one's doubly so — it has been vacant, starved, and hungry for oh, so very long that now—

Impatience. Mr. Woolley (*peremptorily stamping her foot*), give me that heart. Right away—this very instant!

Doll. (*Joyously, getting on his knees before her and holding the heart up.*) Who else more worthy than yourself? I lay my heart, dear Impatience, gladly at your feet. (*Places it on the ground before her.*) From the very first it has been yours. Will you take it?

Impatience. (*Embarrassed.*) Oh, Mr. Woolley, this is so very sudden. (*Aside.*) What an awful complication! I didn't mean it quite this way. (*Aloud.*) Do you really believe you love me?

Doll. This heart is all yours, Impatience. I beg you will not spurn it. See—how beautiful and large it is. Take it in your fair hand and see how warm it is—and all of it is yours, yours, yours forever.

Impatience. (*Aside.*) What shall I do! If I take it I am committed—and what will happen later? If I refuse it—

[*Enter* BABETTE. *She walks to the counter and inspects the register.* WOOLLEY *hastily rises from his knees.* IMPATIENCE *hurriedly picks heart from the floor and thrusts it into her work-basket.*

Impatience. (*Aside.*) Babette! She? She'd flirt with anything. My duty is plain. If I don't take it he'll give it to

59

The Worsted Man

her, and until he is more familiar with the obligations that go with it untold unhappiness may result. I'll not have my Worsted Man a Frankenstein.

Doll. (*Aside to Impatience, ardently.*) Shall you keep it?

Impatience. Yes. (*Aside.*) And later I will tell him 'tis a brother's heart placed in a sister's keeping.

[*Runs off stage.*

Doll. (*Pirouetting gladly.*) Hurrah! I've disposed of one of them. Now for number two. (*Takes a second heart from his pocket and places it softly against his cheek.*) How soft and warm it is. To whom shall I give this choice morsel, I wonder. (*Espies Babette.*) Ah! The very one. Good-morning, Miss Babette. A splendid morning.

Babette. (*Roguishly.*) For games of two, Mr. Woolley. Not for solitaire.

Doll. (*Approaching her and whispering*

in her ear.)   I was just talking about you.

Babette. Me?

Doll. Yes, you.   I was just remarking what beautiful blue eyes you had; what a lovely smile, and how dear and sweet you seemed to be.   Your wealth of golden hair that shimmers in the sun—

Babette. Oh, Mr. Woolley.   (*Aside.*) He's not so bad, after all, even if he hasn't any heart.   (*Aloud.*)   To whom were you saying all these lovely things about me?

Doll. To myself.   To whom else (*seizing her by the hand*) should I confide the secrets of this, my heart? (*Holds it out to her.*)   Such words are too sacred (*getting on his knees*) for any ears but mine—and yours.   Babette, from the first moment I peeped through these shoe-button holes and your loveliness dawned upon my inner excelsior,

I resolved that when I once got a heart it should be yours—and yours alone—

Babette. (*Glancing anxiously about her.*) Oh, do get up, Mr. Woolley. Some one may observe us.

Doll. (*Valiantly.*) And why should they not? To all the world I am ready to proclaim that this heart is thine—

Babette. I admit that I am not indifferent, Mr. Woolley, but are you *sure* it is *all* mine?

Doll. I give it into your keeping—

Babette. (*Kissing him on his forehead and snatching heart from his hands, as she runs gayly off.*) I'll take it—on approval. [*Exit.*

Doll. Gee - whizz! but this is warm work. (*Wiping his brow.*) My forehead is covered with sawdust, I'm perspiring so. (*Pauses and sits down.*) Well, I've worked off two of 'em in great shape. Put the case rather well for an amateur, too. This proposing seems to be a sort of second nature to me. (*Enter* MARIANNA.) Good. Number three approaches. A dainty one at that.

Marianna. Ah, Mr. Woolley — you here?

Doll. Yes, Miss Marianna. Heartsick and hungry for companionship. But why call me *Mr.* Woolley. Is there no less form—formal—

Marianna. (*Demurely.*) I don't know your first name, Mr. Woolley, so how *could* I call you anything else? (*Softly.*) Is it Jack?

Doll. Jack! Jack! Is Jack the name that is written in your heart in letters of fire, Marianna?

Marianna. Well, not exactly that— but it is a name I am awfully fond of.

Doll. It is fate. (*Aside.*) I haven't got any other first name that I know of, so why not Jack? (*Aloud.*) Yes, Marianna, dear, dear Marianna, it is fate. My first name *is* Jack—Jack. I

63

never cared so much for it before—until I knew that *you* liked it. Jack Woolley —that, indeed, is my name. May I not hope to be Jack to you forever?

Marianna. Oh, Mr.—

Doll. Ah, cruel one— Mr. again? Please!

Marianna. Oh, well, then—yes. Jack. I know so little of you, Jack.

Doll. Little of me? Ah, Marianna, what though we met only yesterday, was it not written in the stars when Adam first saw them twinkling in the firmament that my heart was yours, was to wait, wait, wait through all the centuries until you came to claim it? That myriad suns should set, and countless winters pass, and springs galore burst forth in blossoms, yet still should number three—I beg pardon—I mean *this* heart—rest empty till your radiant loveliness came to fill it full with happiness and joy?

The Worsted Man

Marianna. (*Aside.*) Dear me — what beautiful sentiment. (*Aloud.*) You are a poet—er—Jack.

Doll. And like all poets am I a beggar—a beggar at the door of your affections, sweetheart, craving but a crumb of your love if that is all—

Marianna. But where is this heart that you offer, Jack? I am deeply touched.

Doll. (*Pulling it out of his pocket.*) Here! I have kept it safe for you—always for you, Marianna. May I not hope?

Marianna. Well—(*hesitating*)—yes—Jack. You may. Only I must have a little time to look it over. May I—may I take it with me?

Doll. (*Handing her the heart.*) You may—and you may keep it forever, or, if you find you do not wish to, take it hence and bury it deep in some dear spot where some day you may come

65

The Worsted Man

again and let a single tear fall there for
sweet remembrance sake.

> [MARIANNA, *burying her face in her
> handkerchief, takes the heart and
> goes slowly off, sobbing, without
> a word.*

Doll. By Jingo!—that wasn't so easy.
Phew!—but two more like that would
lay me up for a week. Hi—boy.

Bell-Boy. Yassir?

Doll. Bring me a gallon of that water.
I'm pretty nearly done up.

Bell-Boy. Very good, suh.   [*Off.*

> [WOOLLEY *sinks exhausted in his
> chair and closes his eyes, having
> meanwhile taken a fourth heart
> from his pocket. This he places
> on the arm of the chair. As he
> rests, enter* ETHELINDA. *She es-
> pies him apparently sleeping and
> tiptoes softly to his side.*

Ethelinda. (*Clasping her hands and
gazing at him admiringly.*) Ain't he

grand! Something really new at last in men. Oh, if he only *had* a heart! I think I should—but the thought is unmaidenly even for one as old and apparently hopeless as I—thirty-seven last June, but (*coyly*) marked down to twenty-five. (*Giggles, then sighs.*) Ah, me, bargain that I am, I don't— (*She catches sight of the heart.*) But what is this I see? He *has* a heart!

> [DOLL *sighs deeply as* ETHELINDA *reaches out to pick it up. She darts back and hides behind his chair.* DOLL *smiles broadly and winks his eye.*

Doll. (*Stretching his arms and yawning.*) Oh, but I am so tired.

> [*Pretends to doze off again, and a moment later snores.* ETHELINDA *peeps over top of chair, and, seeing him apparently asleep, steals softly back, takes heart in her hand, and kisses it ardently.*

The Worsted Man

Ethelinda. I wonder if I dare steal
it!

[*Looks anxiously about her.* DOLL
*starts up, and rubs his eyes as if
dazed with sleep.* ETHELINDA *hurriedly hides the heart under the
folds of her wrap.*

Doll. Why—is that you, Ethelinda—
or is my dream still going on?

Ethelinda. Your — your dream, Mr.
Woolley?

Doll. Yes, Ethelinda dear. I was
having such a beautiful dream. I
dreamed that you and I were walking
side by side—nay, dear Ethelinda, hand-
in-hand—along a lovely sylvan path together.

Ethelinda. (*Coyly.*) Oh—Mr. Woolley!

Doll. (*Rising and putting his arm
about her waist.*) It was early spring.
The birds were singing—singing always
"Ethelinda." The blossom - scented
breezes blowing through the trees were

68

"WHY—IS THAT YOU, ETHELINDA—OR IS MY
DREAM STILL GOING ON?"

soughing "Ethelinda." Down by the waters of the silver lake the rippling wavelets yapping—I mean lapping—on the virgin sands seemed to whisper "Ethelinda."

Ethelinda. Oh—*Mis*-ter Woolley!

Doll. And then, beloved, we came to a spot where twenty roads spread out in twenty different ways, and finger-posts on each were marked—To HAPPINESS.

Ethelinda. (*Clasping her hands ecstatically.*) Oh—*Mis*—

Doll. But we took none of them, Ethelinda dear. No, said we, we'll go no farther—

Ethelinda. (*Pouting*). But why? Did we not wish for happiness?

Doll. (*Passionately.*) Ah, no, my love, it was not that—we had already found it.

Ethelinda. Oh, ain't you grand! And —er—by-the-way, must I call you *Mr.* Woolley, now?

Doll. Never again, dear. Think of some name you love the best—

Ethelinda. (*Softly.*) *Your* name, whatever it is, is the one I care most for. Is it—Tom?

Doll. Ah! Ah — you dear deceiver, you! Some one must have told you! Yes — Tom — Tom Woolley — homely, but on your lips 'twill seem a poem.

Ethelinda. And I did not need—

Doll. (*Tapping her on the arm.*) To steal my heart? No, dear girl. It was already yours.

> [ETHELINDA *removes heart from her wrap, and, after kissing it ardently, hugs it close.*)

Ethelinda. (*Running off.*) Oh, I am so happy, Tom dear; but I must leave you for a while to read to mother. I'll be back, love, in a little while. Oo won't be too unhappy, will oo, while I'm gone?

The Worsted Man

Doll. I shall be in despair, Ethelinda, but your will is my law.

[*Kisses his hand to her.* ETHELINDA *off.*

Doll. Where in thunder is that boy with the water. Mercy! Four proposals in twenty minutes—that's the record. They are making me work overtime. If things keep on at this rate I'll have to start a Lovers' Union and get a bill through the legislature limiting our working day to eight hours.

[*Enter* BELL-BOY, *with huge pitcher of water.*

Bell-Boy. Here y' are, Mistuh Woolley. Youse'll excuse me, suh, foh sayin' so, but I wouldn't drink mo'n one glass at a time, suh. It's dreadful powahful stuff, suh.

Doll. Thanks for the well-meant advice, my chocolate cream. I have already been warned, but by those who have not properly diagnosed my symptoms. (*Pours out glass of water and drains it.*) Ah! That is refreshing. (*Stiffens up visibly.*) That does put life in one. (*Pours out another and drinks it off. Begins to dance violently.*) Hi! Well, I should think it was powerful stuff, Sambo. Stop me, will you? (*Tries to sit down, but immediately bounces up again and goes pirouetting about the room.*) Stop me, I say.

Bell-Boy. Pahdon me, suh, but I nebber monkies with a buzz-saw, suh. I told you not to drink mo'n one glass, suh. Dis yere condition youse'll have to wuk off foh yo'self, suh.

[*Retires.*

Doll. (*Breathlessly.*) H-how l-lul-long wow-will it t-tut-take for this to wuh-wear off, Sus-sambo?

Bell-Boy. (*From rear.*) Well, I should say yo' might stop dancin' in about ten days, suh.

[*Enter* PRISCILLA *and* PRUDENCE,

72

PRISCILLA *from left* PRUDENCE *from right.*

Priscilla and Prudence. (*Startled by* WOOLLEY'S *activity, which is momentarily increasing.*) Mercy! What has happened, Mr. Woolley?

Doll. (*Two - stepping and seizing* PRUDENCE *in dancing fashion.*) Lul-learning to dance. (*They two-step together.*) I heard you lul-loved dud-dancing, Prudence, dear, and I am learning huh-how juj-just to pup-please please y-you.

Prudence. Well, you have learned very quickly.

Doll. (*Dropping* PRUDENCE *and flying to* PRISCILLA.) Juj-just one turn with you, my heart's desire, and I shall die happy.

[*Seizes her. They make a single turn of the office.*

Priscilla. You dance divinely, Mr. Woolley.

6

The Worsted Man

Doll. (*Dropping* PRISCILLA.) Call me
Bobbie, sweetheart.

Priscilla. What, so soon?

Doll. (*Seizing* PRUDENCE *and dancing.*) Why not? Is not the name of
Prudence written in *my* heart?

Prudence. Your heart?

Doll. (*Taking heart from breast-pocket,
and pressing it into* PRUDENCE'S *hand.*)
It *was* mine—but now it's yours.

[*Drops* PRUDENCE *and dances towards* PRISCILLA.

Prudence. I fear a man so quickly
won may soon be lost. Still, for summer
use he's better than nothing, and he
dances like a dream. [*Exit.*

Doll. (*To* PRISCILLA.) Now that we
are alone, beloved one—

Priscilla. (*Taking arm-chair.*) Pray
sit down, Mr. Woolley.

Doll. Never, dearest, until you breathe
that soft and wondrous yes that tells me
that this heart I offer you (*places it*

74

in her lap as he dances by) is welcome in your eyes. 'Tis just a trifle frayed, perhaps, but that's with ceaseless yearning for thy smile.

Priscilla. (*Inspecting it.*) It *is* a trifle worn, Mr. Woolley. To how many others have you offered it?

Doll. I swear by all that's fair, by your beauteous eyes, by the smile I hope to win, that never in my life before have I offered that heart to any one but you.

Priscilla. (*Doubtfully.*) It seems to have a crack across the middle of it—how came that there?

Doll. It burst for love of you, Priscilla. Pray how else?

Priscilla. (*Demurely.*) H'm! Well— if I'm the one that broke it, then it's mine to mend — but I'm not quite sure—er—

Doll. James — call me James, Priscilla love, and make me the happiest of men.

75

The Worsted Man

Priscilla. I'm not quite sure, James, if I can. But I will try. I've never darned a broken heart before—so I cannot make any rash promises. Will you let me try?

Doll. (*Bowing low and kissing her hand.*) It's all I ask now.

Priscilla. (*Rising.*) I'll go and get my needles.

[*Exit, waving her hand at him smilingly.*

Doll. (*Calming down.*) My, my, my! She was indeed a boon. A wee bit cooler than the rest—she's soothed my agitated nerves. But there still are two to come. Perhaps I might live through one more love affair—but two! I have it, I'll write. (*Sits at small table at left.*) Boy, a pen, paper, and some ink. Also a small bit of wrapping-paper.

Bell-Boy. Yassir.

[*Leans over counter at rear and receives articles from clerk.*

76

Doll. Let's see, what were the names of those two others? I've given a heart to Impatience, one to Babette, one to Marianna, one to Ethelinda, one each to Prudence and Priscilla—that is six. H'm, the others were—oh yes. I remember—Susanna and Janette. I'll send the next to—(*Enter* SUSANNA *with a book in her hand*) — to Janette, for here Susanna is. Good-morning, Miss Susanna.

Susanna. Good-morning, Mr. Woolley. You should not be in-doors this morning —it is such beautiful weather for a walk.

Doll. (*Smiling.*) Is that an invitation?

Susanna. If you choose to take it so. I shall be very glad to show you the links, or the lake, or the twin mountain—

Doll. Oh, indeed — is there a twin mountain?

[BELL-BOY *puts writing materials on table.*

Susanna. Yes — that is, there's one. The other has disappeared during the ages, but all mountain resorts have to have them, you know. Shall we go?

Doll. In a moment, dear. I have a letter to write, and then I am yours.

[*Turns to table and writes.*

Susanna. (*Aside.*) Dear! Well, I like that. There is nothing slow about our worsted cavalier, after all, even if he has no heart, and an imagination made of excelsior.

[*Sits down and reads book.*

Doll. (*Writing.*) Beloved Janette: Where have you been hiding all this lovely morning?

Susanna. (*Looking up.*) Did you speak, Mr. Woolley?

Doll. No, dear—I'm writing out loud, that's all. By-the-way, don't call me Mr. Woolley—it's so very formal. Call me Dick.

Susanna. All right, Dick. Don't hurry. I can wait. [*Resumes reading.*

Doll. (*Writing.*) Don't you know that all the world is bleak and dreary for me, sitting alone without you? Let this my messenger speak for me— my heart, which I send by bearer. If you want it, come to me at once. If you do not, leave it in some deep ravine where it may waste away in hopeless misery. Ever your fond and adoring,

HARRY.

There, I guess that will do for Janette. (*Wraps heart up in paper and addresses note.*) Here boy. (*Whispers.*) Take these to Miss Janette—h'm—let's see, what the deuce is her last name?

Bell-Boy. Barrington, suh.

Doll. Thanks, my ebon social register. What would I do without you? Take these to Miss Barrington, and if you say a word about it to anybody—well, look out for your neck. I might mistake

The Worsted Man

it for the bell, my darkling Cupid, and
ring it, don't you see.

ell-Boy. I'm on, suh.   [*Off.*

Doll. And now, my dear Susanna, let
us hie ourselves to the weeping summit
of the solitary twin.

> [SUSANNA *closes her book and, rising,*
> *takes* WOOLLEY'S *arm. They go*
> *out laughing gayly. As they dis-*
> *appear* IMPATIENCE *enters hur-*
> *riedly from the other side.*

Impatience. Where is he? I am
simply worried to death about this
heart. Where *did* he get it and what
notions—

> [*Enter* BABETTE, PRUDENCE, PRIS-
> CILLA, *and* MARIANNA *from dif-*
> *ferent sides.*

*Marianna, Babette, Prudence, and
Priscilla.* Where's Mr. Woolley?

> [ETHELINDA *puts her head in at the*
> *door, coyly.*

Ethelinda. Tom—Tom dear. (*Enters.*)

Why, where's my— (*Spies the others.*)
Oh—hullo girls. What's become of Mr.
Woolley?

[*Enter* JANETTE, *waving letter in her
   hand.*

Janette. What's that to you? He's
mine. I've won him.

Omnes. You?

Janette. Yes—here's his letter and
there's—his heart. [*Holds them out.*

Impatience. (*Snatching letter from her
hand and reading it.*) Oh, the villain!

Ethelinda. Ain't he *awful.* [*Weeps.*

The Rest. (*Indignantly.*) The flirt.
He made love to me.

[*Enter* SUSANNA, *still holding* MR.
   WOOLLEY'S *arm.*

Susanna. (*Joyously.*) Girls, congratu-
late me. I have won the prize.

All. You?

Susanna. Yes — me. Mr. Woolley
—Dick—dear old Dick, has given me
his heart.

The Worsted Man

[DOLL *takes centre of stage and looks sheepishly around.*
All. (*Glancing angrily at him.*) Villain, dastard, flirt!
Doll. (*Nervously.*) Let me explain—
Impatience. (*Firmly.*) There is no explanation possible, you wicked man. Have you not given your heart to each one of us?
Doll. Yes, but—
Impatience. Then you must pay the penalty.

CHORUS: GIRLS

(*Music: "Now Is Not This Ridiculous," from "Patience."*)

Now is not he preposterous, and is not
    he unduteous,
  An unalloyed philanderer, a wicked,
    wicked man!
He's courted us in language that was
    chosen well and beauteous,
  No lover's put it better since this life
    of ours began,

"THEN YOU MUST PAY THE PENALTY"

The Worsted Man

Yet while his words were cheering us,
Flirtatiously was fleering us,
    Winking at us, blinking at us, on the
    Mormon plan.
Yes actually fleering at us, peering at
    us, sneering at us,
    Pretty sort of treatment from this
    wicked worsted man.
    Pretty sort of treatment from this
    wicked worsted man.

    [*They all rush madly at* DOLL,
    *who cowers before them, and each
    seizing hold of a worsted end they
    begin pulling him to pieces.*
    WOOLLEY *writhes as the worsted
    unravels, and the stage goes dark.
    A moment later the stage lighting
    up again discloses girls all weep-
    ing in semicircle, except* IM-
    PATIENCE, *who stands like an
    avenging goddess over a huge heap
    of worsted ravellings, mittens,
    shoes, and the face of* WOOLLEY—

The Worsted Man

all that is left of the Worsted Man.

CHORUS

(*Same as Opening Chorus.*)
Seven lone lorn maidens we,
Not a man to ease our woe.
All the season we shall be
Seven lone lorn maidens—oh!

IMPATIENCE

Love feeds on hope, they say, but hope
is dead.

ALL

Ah, miserie!

IMPATIENCE

Hope ne'er can overcome flirtation
dread.

ALL

Ah, miserie!

IMPATIENCE

Alas for us! We sit and sadly plan—

84

The Worsted Man

ALL
Ah, miserie!

IMPATIENCE
Once more a summer Eden without man.

ALL
Ah, miserie!

CHORUS
All our love is wasted quite,
   All our yearnings gone for naught.
Mr. Woolley was not quite
   Such a person as we sought.

ALL
Ah, miserie!

SOLO: IMPATIENCE
(To Woolley's remains.)
Oh glancing eyes
   Thy glancing all is wasted.

85

The Worsted Man

Go, Mormon heart,
   The sweets of love untasted!
O Worsted Man,
   What boots my anxious scheming,
When I awake
   To find it idle dreaming.

ALL

Ah, miserie!

CURTAIN

Reprint Publishing

FOR PEOPLE WHO GO FOR ORIGINALS.

This book is a facsimile reprint of the original edition. The term refers to the facsimile with an original in size and design exactly matching simulation as photographic or scanned reproduction.

Facsimile editions offer us the chance to join in the library of historical, cultural and scientific history of mankind, and to rediscover.

The books of the facsimile edition may have marks, notations and other marginalia and pages with errors contained in the original volume. These traces of the past refers to the historical journey that has covered the book.

ISBN 978-3-95940-066-4

Facsimile reprint of the original edition
Copyright © 2015 Reprint Publishing
All rights reserved.

www.reprintpublishing.com

www.ingramcontent.com/pod-product-compliance
Lightning Source LLC
Chambersburg PA
CBHW070827250626

47170CB00006B/2244

* 9 7 8 3 9 5 9 4 0 0 6 6 4 *